The Bird Who Was an Elephant

BY

Aleph Kamal

PAINTINGS BY

Frané Lessac

J. B. LIPPINCOTT · NEW YORK

It was still early when the Bird flew in from the desert. But already the village was being brought to a boil by the rays of the Sun.

Down in the middle of the river, women bathers were saluting the Sun, laughing and splashing. From the Bird's height, the red and green and yellow saris seemed like beautiful flowers, floating among the lotuses and lilies.

The Bird swooped down into the river for a cool dip.

The village street was getting busy. The shops seemed to stand at attention, side by side, their doors thrown open wide, all showing off their wares. The sweetmeat seller, the tailor, the dentist, the jeweler and the moneylender.

The Bird perched over the spice shop, breathing the wonderful smells of ginger, nutmeg, coriander…oh, so many smells!

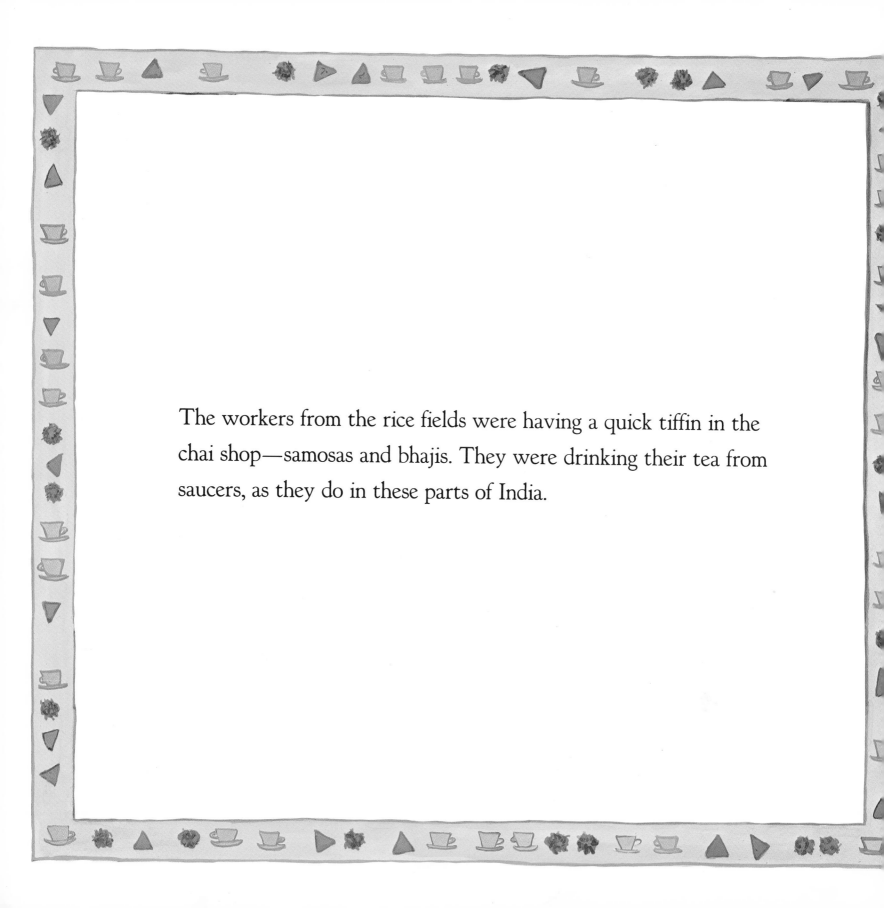

The workers from the rice fields were having a quick tiffin in the chai shop—samosas and bhajis. They were drinking their tea from saucers, as they do in these parts of India.

On the top story of the chai shop was the Palmist's sign. For only five rupees the Palmist would study your hand and tell you your past—and your future. For ten rupees, he could tell you what your past lives had been and what your future ones would be.

The Bird flew in through the Palmist's window.

"O Palmist, how can you tell these things?"

"Your palm is a map of your life, so I can see what has happened and what will come about."

"O Palmist, I have no money, but please tell me what I was two thousand years ago!"

"Let's see. Give me your right claw."

The Palmist measured one line of the claw carefully.

"Two thousand years ago, you were an Elephant. Your job was to carry children on your back across the gardens of a Maharajah's palace."

The Bird could not understand how a big Elephant could change into a small Bird.

"How long will I remain a Bird?"

"Not for very long," the Palmist answered. "Everything changes."

"And what will I be next time?"

"A Fish in the sea," replied the Palmist. Then he added, "That will be all for today."

"Thank you!" called the Bird as it flew out into the street again.

The street was alive with sound. A love song played on the radio. A bullock cart carrying a farmer and his load of onions and potatoes creaked slowly toward the marketplace. The beggar woman and her two children dressed in rags came walking past, holding out their hands for baksheesh, telling their sad story to the world.

Farther down the street a Sacred Cow with a garland of orange marigolds around her neck was meditating.

"I'm back," said the Bird. "What's new in these parts?"

The Sacred Cow said nothing. Her large brown eyes stared into the dry distance.

It is said that the Wise use words sparingly.

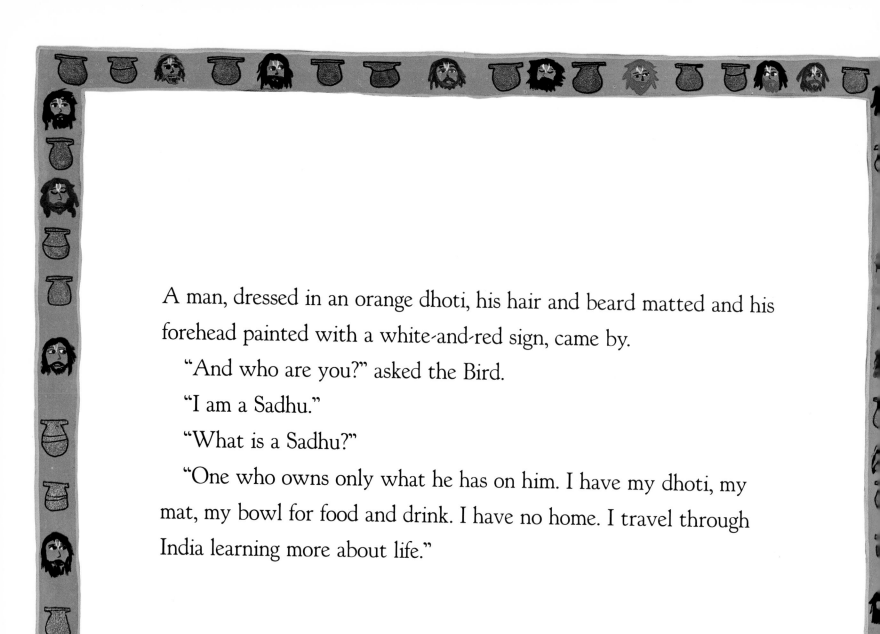

A man, dressed in an orange dhoti, his hair and beard matted and his forehead painted with a white-and-red sign, came by.

"And who are you?" asked the Bird.

"I am a Sadhu."

"What is a Sadhu?"

"One who owns only what he has on him. I have my dhoti, my mat, my bowl for food and drink. I have no home. I travel through India learning more about life."

A few villagers were gathering around the Snake Charmer. The Snake was doing a lazy dance to the tune of the Charmer's flute.

"I'm back," said the Bird.

"Namaste," said the Snake. "Long time no see....Join me later for tiffin?"

"I have another d-d-date," the Bird replied nervously, and flew off in the opposite direction.

The land was steaming under the Sun and the Bird was hungry and hot. The Bird drank water from a dripping tap. The water tasted good.

While the fruit and vegetable walli was busy bargaining with a housewife, the Bird pecked at a date and then at a banana. But the walli noticed, and clapped her hands loudly at the Bird. The Bird flapped away....

The Sun was slipping westward away from the village. Outside the chai shop the Sacred Cow was demanding a chapati. Then another.

The train from the mountains moved into the station, its coaches crammed with people, like tightly packed flowers. The steam engine puffed smoke into the air. A man on the platform was selling tea in clay cups. The stationmaster was filling out a form. Some children waved at the Bird. A Sadhu once said that if you waited at a railway station for one whole day and a night, you would see the world unfold in front of you.

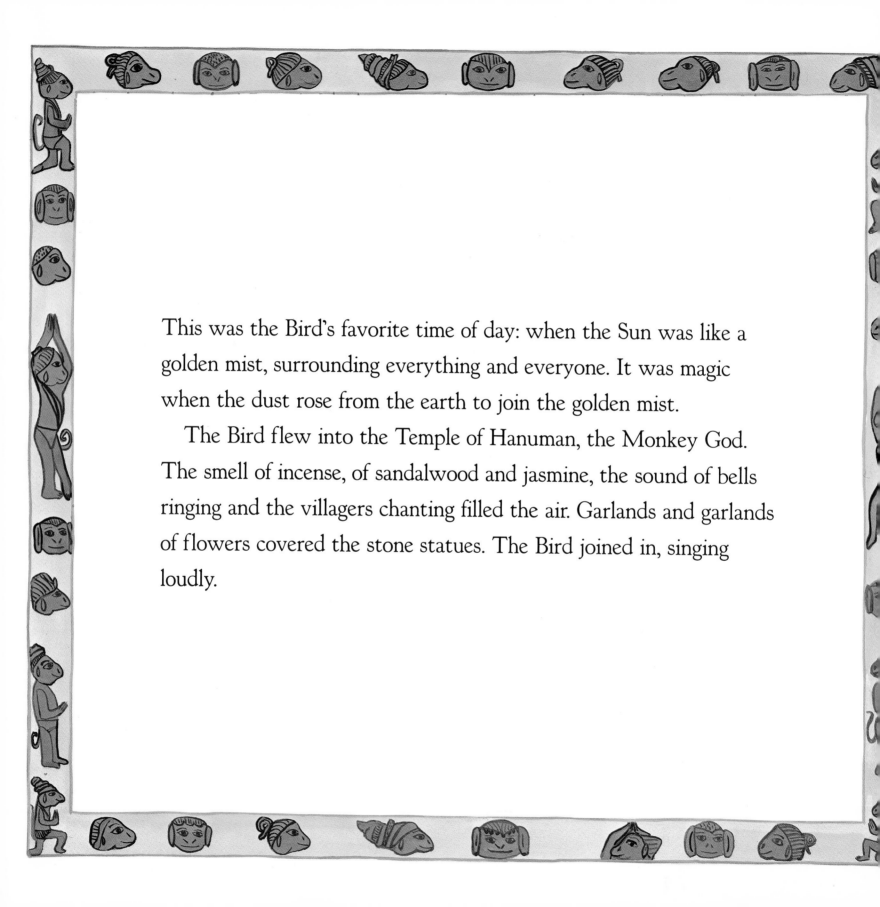

This was the Bird's favorite time of day: when the Sun was like a golden mist, surrounding everything and everyone. It was magic when the dust rose from the earth to join the golden mist.

The Bird flew into the Temple of Hanuman, the Monkey God. The smell of incense, of sandalwood and jasmine, the sound of bells ringing and the villagers chanting filled the air. Garlands and garlands of flowers covered the stone statues. The Bird joined in, singing loudly.

Outside the temple, peacocks were still parading on the ground. Monkeys were chattering and quarreling over who would sleep where.

The Bird, too, had to find a resting place in a tree somewhere. The Moon, slowly, was finding her way across the darkening sky. The Night hushed down all sound and noise. Three rats danced and played in the moonlight.

The Bird was tired.

But it was good to be home.

To the children of India, for the children of the West
including Jake, Luke, Michael, Mistral…

A Note From the Author

A *sari* is a large piece of cloth that an Indian woman wears as a long dress • A *walli* is a woman who sells things • A *dhoti* is a piece of cloth worn by an Indian man instead of pants • A *rupee* is Indian money • *Baksheesh* means a gift • *Tiffin* is a tea break • *Samosas* are small triangle-shaped vegetable pastries • *Bhajis* are round-shaped snacks made of vegetables • A *chapati* is a flat pancake like bread • *Namaste* means Welcome; Indians use it to say hello and good-bye.

And how could a bird have been an elephant? Hindus in India believe that we have many lives and that when we die we can become another human being—or an animal.

The Bird Who Was An Elephant. Text copyright © 1989 by Aleph Kamal. Illustrations copyright © 1989 by Frané Lessac. First published by Cambridge University Press, U.K. All rights reserved. Printed in the United States of America. For information address J.B. Lippincott Junior Books, 10 East 53rd Street, New York, N.Y. 10022.
Typography by Andrew Rhodes   1 2 3 4 5 6 7 8 9 10   First American Edition, 1990

Library of Congress Cataloging-in-Publication Data
Kamal, Aleph. The bird who was an elephant / Aleph Kamal ; paintings by Frané Lessac.
    p.   cm.
    Summary: A bird visits a colorful village in India, seeing a spice shop, a sacred cow, a snake charmer, and a palmist.
    ISBN 0-397-32445-6 : $. — ISBN 0-397-32446-4 (lib. bdg.) :
$
    [1. India—Fiction. 2. Birds—Fiction.] I. Lessac, Frané, ill.
II. Title.
PZ7.K1266Bi 1990   89-14536
[E]—dc20   CIP AC